FOREST FEELINGS

SALLY THE SKUNK FEELS SCARED

by Megan Atwood
illustrated by Carissa Harris

GRASSHOPPER

Tools for Parents & Teachers

Grasshopper Books enhance imagination and introduce the earliest readers to fiction with fun storylines and illustrations. The easy-to-read text supports early reading experiences with repetitive sentence patterns and sight words.

Before Reading

- Discuss the cover illustration. What do they see?
- Look at the picture glossary together. Discuss the words.

Read the Book

- Read the book to the child, or have him or her read independently.
- "Walk" through the book and look at the illustrations. Who is the main character? What is happening in the story?

After Reading

- Prompt the child to think more. Ask: Sally feels scared. How do we know? What does she say and do that show she is afraid?

Grasshopper Books are published by Jump!
5357 Penn Avenue South
Minneapolis, MN 55419
www.jumplibrary.com

Library of Congress Cataloging-in-Publication Data

Names: Atwood, Megan, author.
Harris, Carissa, illustrator.
Title: Sally the skunk feels scared / by Megan Atwood; illustrated Carissa Harris.
Description: Minneapolis, MN: Jump!, Inc., 2024.
Series: Forest feelings | Includes index.
Audience: Ages 7–10.
Identifiers: LCCN 2023029049 (print)
LCCN 2023029050 (ebook)
ISBN 9798889969723 (hardcover)
ISBN 9798889969730 (paperback)
ISBN 9798889969747 (ebook)
Subjects: CYAC: Fear—Fiction. | Thunderstorms—Fiction.
Skunks—Fiction. | LCGFT: Animal fiction. | Picture books.
Classification: LCC PZ7.A8952 Sal 2024 (print)
LCC PZ7.A8952 (ebook)
DDC [E] —dc23
LC record available at https://lccn.loc.gov/2023029049
LC ebook record available at https://lccn.loc.gov/2023029050

Editor: Jenna Gleisner
Direction and Layout: Molly Ballanger
Illustrator: Carissa Harris

Printed in the United States of America at
Corporate Graphics in North Mankato, Minnesota.

Table of Contents

A Scary Feeling Passes

Sally the skunk and her siblings smell flowers in the meadow. Sally loves the different colors and smells.

Sally smells something else.
Her heart beats faster.

"It's starting to rain!" Sally says. "We should go!"

Her sister Laurel says, "I love rain."

Her brother Daniel nods. "It's fun to play in!"

But Sally does not like the rain. She knows that it can mean a thunderstorm is coming.

Sally remembers the last thunderstorm. The thunder was so loud it shook the whole den. It scared Sally.

Sally starts shaking. She wants to run but feels frozen. She feels frozen in her thoughts, too.

"What's wrong, Sally?" Laurel asks.

Just then, lightning flashes.

Thunder booms.

The sound startles Sally.

Sally runs until she reaches the den.

She closes her eyes tight
and covers her ears.

Then she hears laughing.

"Come out!" Laurel says. "The storm is passing!"

"Thunder is just noise, Sally. It can't hurt you," Daniel adds.

Laurel and Daniel are OK in the rain. Maybe she could be, too, Sally thinks. She takes a deep breath and crawls out. She hears thunder but nothing bad happens.

The rain feels good on Sally's face. Her heart beats slower. Her body stops shaking.

Daniel and Laurel grab Sally's paws. "Let's play!" they say.

Sally doesn't feel afraid anymore. Just like the storm, her scary feelings passed!

Let's Review!

Look at the scenes below. Point to those that show Sally scared. How do you know?